Emily Barr is the well-lo[v...] of *Backpack*, the origina[...] many other highly acc[...] journalist, she has travelled around the world and written columns and travel pieces for the *Observer* and the *Guardian*. After living in France, Emily and her husband (whom she met backpacking) settled in Cornwall with their three children. To learn more about Emily and her novels, you can visit her website www.emilybarr.com.

Praise for Emily Barr's novels:

'We can't praise Emily Barr's novels enough; they're fresh, original and hugely readable'
Glamour

'A real page-turner with a plot twist worthy of *Lost*'
Cosmopolitan

'A characteristically dark-hued tale, with unexpected twists'
Guardian

'Beautifully written with engaging, emotionally complex characters and a great plot. I couldn't put it down'
Daily Mail

'Compelling'
Heat

By Emily Barr

Blackout

EMILY BARR

headline
review

First published in 2013 by Headline Review
An imprint of Headline Publishing Group

2

Cataloguing in Publication Data is available from the British Library

ISBN 978 1 4722 1248 1

Typeset by Palimpsest Book Production Ltd, Falkirk, Stirlingshire

Printed and bound by CPI Group (UK) Ltd, Croydon, CR0 4YY

Headline's policy is to use papers that are natural, renewable and
recyclable products and made from wood grown in sustainable forests.
The logging and manufacturing processes are expected to conform to
the environmental regulations of the country of origin.

HEADLINE PUBLISHING GROUP
An Hachette UK Company
338 Euston Road
London NW1 3BH

www.headline.co.uk
www.hachette.co.uk

Blackout

As soon as I wake up I know I am going to be sick.

The room is blurry and I am woozy. My head hurts. Everything is fuzzy around the edges. I cannot think. There is no space in my brain for anything except the sickness and my head, which hurts so much that I think it might have an axe or a knife sticking out of it.

I roll over. I have to get to the bathroom.

I am ill. I have become ill in the night. I am going to be sick. That is all. It is the only thing in the world right now.

Daylight makes my head pound. I try to stand up, but I cannot make my legs move the way I want them to. The wall jumps forward, and then so does the floor, and I feel myself land on it.

I fell out of bed because my legs didn't work.

1

That is almost funny, except that it is so scary it takes my breath away.

Then the vomit comes. I cannot do anything other than turn my head. My stomach heaves and contracts, and the liquid gathers on the floorboards and then starts dripping down the cracks between them. That is awful, but also weird, as the bedroom floor should have a carpet. We don't have floorboards in the bedroom. There is a wooden floor in the sitting room, but I was in bed. Things come slowly into focus. The edges of them sharpen.

This is not my bedroom. It is nothing like my bedroom. It is a strange room with a bed in it. The light coming through the window is bright. The ceiling is sloping like an attic.

I close my eyes and drift back to sleep, lying on the floor in a puddle of my own sick.

Chapter 1

Inside

The next time I open my eyes I have forgotten all over again. Again I think I am at home. I still feel weird and ill. This time, though, I wake lying on the floor with my face and half my hair caked in dried sick. The smell of it makes me retch and I am nearly sick all over again.

I struggle to sit up, trying to make sense of this. I am in someone's attic. I have never been here before. I need water and, when I manage to pull myself up and look round, I see that there is a basin in the corner of the room, with a glass.

I make it as far as sitting on the bed, staring at the basin. I will have to see if my legs are working. If I can get there, I can drink and rinse my hair. I take a deep breath.

I smell some air beyond the sick, and it smells strange. It is not like the air at home. This is the air of a place I do not know. It is warm and breezy. I lie back on the bed and close my eyes and try to remember where I am, and how I got here, and what has happened.

I went to bed in my own bedroom, exactly as normal. I remember it clearly. I live in London, and I went to bed after Rob. I got into bed next to him and went to sleep. That is what happened last night.

Yet I cannot have gone to sleep in one room and woken up in another.

This should be a dream, but I know that it isn't. My eyes are sore. Everything about me is wobbly and unstable. I pinch my arm, because that is what you do if you think you're dreaming, but it hurts, and my nails leave little crescents in my skin.

Time passes. I get up and stumble to the basin. Here, the ceiling slopes too much for me to stand up straight. There is no furniture except the bed, and oddly I seem to have nothing with me. No bag, no purse.

I drink three glasses of water quickly, and then hold on to the edge of the basin and wait for the sudden sick feeling to pass. I splash my face until the dried vomit has gone, and I do my best to rinse my hair, which sticks wetly to the side of my face. The walls are white and peeling with damp in some places. Red and white checked curtains flap in the breeze. There are sounds coming from outside. They are sounds of cars and horns, raised voices.

Suddenly I notice that I am fully dressed – but in clothes I have never seen before. They are far nicer than my own clothes, and they fit me perfectly. I am wearing a stiff cotton dress and a cardigan. The dress is white and green. The cardigan is green too, the kind of tight one that Audrey Hepburn might have worn. I am more confused than ever. Normally I wear jeans and T-shirts and anything I happen to find in a charity shop. I am not myself any more.

I go to the window, my new dress swishing as I walk properly now, and pull back the curtains.

This is, of course, an attic. I am at the top of a tall building, leaning out of the window and seeing a straight drop down to a street below. There are cars and people down there, shops at ground level and windows like mine further up. The building opposite is grand, with wrought-iron bars around the windowsills and painted wooden shutters. It goes straight up like a mountain. It is far away, across a wide street.

The cars are driving on the wrong side of the road.

*

A search of the room confirms that I have no phone, no bag, no purse, no money. I check my strange new clothes for pockets, but I know already that they don't have any.

I wonder whether I have time-travelled, whether I am somehow in a different era. I am wearing clothes from the forties. Perhaps I am in the forties? Or perhaps I am in the after-life? I could have died. I might be in a coma, and this could be the world my mind has created for me. That seems more likely than any other explanation.

The door is closed, and I run to it, suddenly certain that I will find I am locked in. However, it opens quickly and easily, and I am on a landing. There is a door opposite mine. I try the handle but it is locked. I see a wooden staircase that I start down, holding the handrail, my shaky legs creaking every step of the way.

I run down staircases, across landings, down the next flight, across more, and finally I am in a gloomy hallway, tiled in black and white checks. Dust drifts around in the light that slants down from a small pane of glass above the top of the door.

I pause before I pull it open. I have no idea what I am going to find.

Chapter 2

Paris. Outside

It is not London. It is not in Britain. This is not a place I have ever been to before. The cars are driving on the other side of the road, and their number plates are most definitely foreign.

I let the door slam shut behind me, then realise how stupid that was. That room was the only place I had. I turn back and try the door handle, but it does not open.

I cannot be lost on the streets of a strange city with nothing at all. I bang on the door, but that just hurts my hand. There is a bank of buzzers beside the door – five of them on top of one another, with numbers next to them – and I press them in order. One, two, three, four, five, over and over again. I stand right up next to the intercom, but nobody answers. No one comes in. No one goes out. I cannot climb the outside of the building to crawl in through the attic window, and none of the lower windows are open, so I will have to do something else.

Nobody walking past takes any notice of me. It occurs to me that if I am a ghost, they might not be able to see me. I walk into someone on purpose, a man with a fat stomach that bulges over the top of his trousers. He says something to me in what I think is French, then frowns, hitches his stomach so it lurches upwards and walks on.

'Sorry,' I say, but he ignores that.

I am visible, then. I exist. My head is pounding and I am desperately thirsty, as well as hungry. I thought it was morning when I woke up, but now I am not so sure. It could be any time. I set off down the road, turning back to stare at the doorway so I will remember where it is. The number 246 is on the door. If nothing changes, I will come back later and press those buzzers again.

'I am Sophie,' I say, aloud. I need to fix myself into some sort of reality. 'My name is Sophie Mayes.' I run through the facts in my head. 'I live in London. I have a partner, Rob, and . . .'

I knew there was something I had forgotten. I have a baby. I need my baby. But I cannot remember his name. He is a boy. His name is either Arthur or Harry. My head spins. I have no idea which name is his.

I have to get to him. I've forgotten his name, but I remember his smell, his soft hair, his laugh. He loves me and I love him. I need to find him. I start to run.

I pass trees with trunks dotted with sunlight and bright green leaves high above me. I run through sun and shade, over patches of sandy soil, the sun hot on my head, and soon I am in a place that would be a town square if it weren't a triangle. A café has tables outside, and people are sitting around eating bread out of baskets, and pastries, and drinking juice and coffee from little cups.

I search frantically for a pay phone. No one uses phone boxes any more. I want to ask someone if I can use their mobile, but I know they wouldn't let me, and I don't even have the words to ask. I get lost – completely, hopelessly lost – though as I am already lost, it doesn't matter.

I wish I had done French at school. I wish I had listened for the year or two that I did study it.

In the end I find a phone on a wall in the shade of a small leafy tree.

The phone is sticky, and I do not understand any of the instructions. I have no idea how to make a phone call without money. In the end, I manage it by calling the numbers written on the instructions until I get through to the operator.

'I want to make a reverse charge call,' I shout, and the sound of my voice startles me. We go through a few details and, in the end, there is a British ringtone.

It rings and rings. I wait for Rob to pick up. He has to answer. He has to. I want to hear the baby chatting in the background. I want Rob to sigh and laugh and explain why I am here, and where this is.

'You went to a hen party,' he might say. 'You got new clothes. How can you have forgotten? How much did you drink last night? Have you been sick?'

'Yes,' I would say, and everything would be all right.

Nobody answers. The answer machine should have got it by now. It always kicks in after five rings. I often miss calls because I can't find a handset. Five rings is not very long and the machine is better at getting things done than I am. It is never switched off. Never.

But today everything is wrong, and I should

not be surprised. Rob is not at home. My baby boy is not at home. Unless he is home on his own, crying as the phone rings and rings.

I can picture it so clearly I am sure it is happening.

The operator comes back to tell me there's no answer, but I slam the phone down and run. Today is Monday. He goes to nursery on Monday. Perhaps he is in nursery. I need to find out where I am, and get myself home.

I run into a newsagent's. A woman looks up at me, bored. She has black hair and too much blusher, and she is wearing a shapeless white dress over a very skinny body. She could be forty, or sixty-five.

'Paris?' I ask her, pointing at the floor. *'Am I in Paris?'*

She smiles with one side of her mouth.

'Yes,' she says, in heavily accented English. She laughs, and I can see her wanting to ask me how I could not know. 'Yes, this is Paris.' Then she says the word in French, 'Paree.'

I screw my eyes tight shut and try, again, to remember how I got here. It is no use. I have never been to Paris in my life, and I went to sleep in my own bed last night. I did not come on a hen party or anything else. Yet here I am.

11

I suddenly wonder.

'Monday?' I ask. 'Morning?'

She shakes her head, and comes out from behind the counter to scan the papers. When she has found the one she is looking for, she puts it in front of my face and points. It is a paper called the *International Herald Tribune*, and it is in English.

'Here,' she says, pointing to the date. 'This is today. Not Monday.'

We both look at it.

It seems that today is Thursday.

Chapter 3

London. A year ago

He stood in the doorway, looked at her lying on her back, and laughed.

'What the hell are you doing?' he said. He walked over to the stereo, which was playing classical music very loudly, and turned it down.

She tried not to laugh. She was stretched out so far that her feet were under the coffee table, while her fingertips reached the bookcase. It was not really a flat that had space for a pregnant woman to lie down on the floor.

'Turn it back up,' she said, in a loud whisper. 'I'm making the baby clever.'

'Right.' He nodded and came to sit on the sofa, looking down at his heavily pregnant partner lying on the floor. He did not turn the music back up. 'Can I help? Six sixes are thirty-six! Should I speak to him in French?'

'Him *or her*. And no. Maybe one of the Asian languages.'

'Hmm. I'd have to learn one first. What are we going to do if this baby is cleverer than we are?'

She laughed. 'Our genius child will teach us things.'

They were both excited about the baby's arrival. It was due in seventeen days, and Sophie was preparing herself frantically. She listened to classical music because she had read that it would make the baby clever. Even though she knew it was unlikely, really, to be true, she still felt it was worth a try. It was not going to do any harm, anyway.

She sat down by candlelight with her legs as close to crossed as she could get them, and sent peaceful, happy thoughts to the child who was preparing to be born. 'Welcome, my darling,' she said, in her head. The words did not need to leave her body, because both she and the baby were living inside it. She went to pregnancy yoga classes and to swimming, to every class she could find.

She was going to be the best mother in the world. Rob was going to be the best father. Every time she doubted herself, she remembered her own mother. That made her strong. All she had to do, to be the best mother in the world, was the exact opposite of everything her own mother had ever done. That was the formula. It was simple. Her own mother was the worst mother in the world, so Sophie was going to do things differently, and be the best.

Her best friend Jess had two girls. Jess told Sophie she could do it, and Sophie was starting to believe her.

That evening they sat on the sofa, the way they often sat, with Rob leaning on the sofa's arm, and Sophie and her bump between his legs. His hands reached around the sides of her, on to the bump. Occasionally the baby would kick. They loved it when that happened.

'Look at us,' he said with a laugh, and she looked at the big mirror that was balanced against the fireplace, too heavy to be fixed to the wall with its crumbly plaster.

She was thirty-three, and she was pregnant. That in itself was odd when she stopped to think about it. She was going to have a baby, even though she remembered, at the age of nine, telling the world that this was something that would never happen.

'I won't be a mummy,' she had said, sucking a strand of hair. 'Not ever.'

'Good idea,' her own mother had said. 'It's boring. And you can't change your mind and put them back. That's for sure.'

Sophie's mum, Sandra, was angry with every-thing, but most of all with Sophie. Sandra was small and wiry and full of hate. It had taken Sophie years to see that other people's mothers were not like that. The nice mums baffled her, and she knew she would not know how to be one, and that this meant she could never have a child.

Then she met Rob, a PE teacher with broad shoulders and a loud and wonderful laugh. Rob wanted a baby more than most women did, and he wanted it with her. He wanted a boy called Arthur and a girl called Stella. With his support she started to feel she might be able to do it. Even so, she said no for two years until she saw that he was about to leave her, because it was so important to him. Then she decided that she could do it.

'I don't have to be like my own mother,' she had said aloud.

He had laughed. 'Bloody hell! Please don't be! Be yourself, Soph.'

And then it had become so simple. This was her baby, hers and Rob's. They were going to do it properly. Now she was sitting there, her long hair tied up in a messy bunch, with Rob, the love of her life, sitting behind her with his strong arms around her, and their adored baby waiting to be born.

'I love you,' she said, and the 'you' was plural. Rob understood that at once.

'We know,' he replied.

Chapter 4

Paris

It is Thursday.

The day that should be Monday is actually Thursday. Even at my worst I never lost three whole days. Nobody loses three days. It is not possible. Days come one after the other, from the day you're born until the day you die. If you stay in bed for a day, the day still happens. If you black out in a coma or something, you wake up in hospital. You do not wake up in a mysterious room in Paris.

I went to bed at home on Sunday. Monday, Tuesday and Wednesday have happened, and I have no idea what I did. I search my mind for a memory but I do not find even a shred of one. I cannot drag up a single moment of any one of those three days.

I know that something awful has happened. It is a thing so huge and so bad that I can only

17

see its shape, hovering above me. It is around me like a cloud, above me, behind me, in front of me. It is everywhere around me, but nowhere else.

The sun is shining. Other people probably like that. I might have liked it, once. I start to run.

The phone did not work. I need to get myself home, to run to our flat and bang on the door, or break a window, to find my baby. I need to find my family. Something has happened to us all.

There is only one thing I can possibly do, and that is to get home. That means I need to go to the police. I don't want to – I want to keep away from them whenever possible, because they scare me – but as far as I know, I haven't done anything wrong. I should find the nearest police station, and walk in there and ask for someone who speaks English.

I might be missing. The police might all be looking for me. If I found a British paper, my face might be on the front of it. As I have this thought, I pass a huge stand of papers outside a newsagent's shop.

I look through the papers. There is a *Mail*, a *Guardian*, a *Times*. I snatch them up, one by one, but I am not on the front of any of them. I flick through the *Mail*, but I reach the business news and know there is nothing about me in there at all.

It is not possible that no one could be looking for me. I have a family. People would know that I had gone.

I reach the river and see the Eiffel Tower on the other side of it. It is black and tall, pointing up at the pale blue sky, and could not be anything else. That proves, at least, that I really am in Paris. I run across a bridge towards it. This takes longer than I expected. Then, on the Left Bank, I stop someone at random, and say: 'Police?'

I sit down while they look for a particular person who speaks fluent English. The policeman I speak to first has a bristly moustache, and he disapproves of my total lack of French. I sit in a corner of a dark room, on a plastic chair, and try to work out exactly what to say.

If they speak to the British police, they will find out the darkest thing about me. Then they will look at me and they will know what kind of woman lurks inside me. I cannot bear it. I try to sit still and tell myself that this is my best way of getting home, but what if it's not? What have I done on those lost days? What if the police are the very worst people for me to go to?

I sit there and hear the seconds tick by on the old-fashioned clock on the wall. Its second hand leaps forward each time, looking as if it is expecting something exciting to happen. When I have counted forty-five more clicks, I stand up and walk, then run, out of the building.

Some people walk past, in the direction of the Eiffel Tower, and I hear that they are speaking English. Immediately I turn and walk back to them.

They are a family: two adults, two children. I think the children are about four and six. Something like that, anyway. The dad is very tall and skinny and the mum looks friendly, in jeans and a T-shirt with sunglasses on her head and hair in a ponytail.

'Hi,' I say. 'Are you English?'

The woman smiles and glances at her husband. 'Yes.' She sounds wary, and I try to arrange my face to look less tense. It is difficult.

'Is there a problem?' says the husband. I watch the girl take her mother's hand and attempt to pull her along. I have no idea how to explain myself.

'I need to get to the station,' I tell them. 'To get home. I don't know why I'm here. I need to get to my baby. Could I use your phone? Could I . . . Where's the station? I need my baby. The station with the train to England? Can I borrow your phone?'

That did not come out the way I wanted it to.

'Is it an emergency?' says the man. 'We can direct you to the station, of course.'

'Use my phone,' the woman says, and she hands it to me quickly, looking up at her husband and then away again.

I grab it. I can see him opening his mouth to tell me to give it back.

'Thanks!'

It is an iPhone. I put in Rob's mobile number and press the call button. It rings a few times, and then it suddenly stops. It doesn't go to voicemail. It just cuts out.

They are looking at me, all four of them. I try to take a deep breath, but instead I burst into tears. People are walking past us, mainly tourists. An older woman, wearing black, looks concerned, but doesn't stop. Most people ignore me.

21

'Hey,' the woman says, and she puts her arm around my shoulder.

I try to sniff my tears back, but once I start it is hard to stop. I still feel sick. My head still hurts. I have lost my family, and I am very, very scared. I bury my head in her shoulder and sob. For a long time I cannot stop.

'It's OK,' I manage to say. 'I just need to get home.'

'I'll show you the way to the station,' says the man, but he is impatient and keen to get away. I am annoying him.

'Thanks,' I say.

'Well,' he tells me briskly. 'You need to cross this bridge. And then walk north.' I try to listen. He ends by saying, 'And then you can buy a ticket and go home.'

I have no money, and no passport.

Chapter 5

London. A year ago

When labour started, she was thrilled. After days of trying to convince herself that each twinge was a contraction, she knew it when it happened. This was it. This time she did not call Rob at work, did not check her hospital bag. The bag was packed. It had been packed for weeks. She knew that it had everything in it that was needed, and plenty more besides. It was crammed with classical music CDs and healthy snacks, the long birth plan, baby books and all the things she was going to need. In a linen bag inside it, to keep them perfect, were the baby's clothes. Arthur or Stella was going to wear white. There were tiny white suits and soft white cardigans. There were cloth nappies, and no bottles. The baby would not wear disposable nappies, and he or she would not drink from a bottle.

She smiled at the bag, and paced around the

flat, calm. She tidied the kitchen, lined up the mugs in the cupboard and then cleaned the tiny bathroom (the baby bath was standing on end in a corner, waiting). She brushed her hair, and checked the time. Then she put the TV on and sat down on the floor to see what would happen.

Three hours later, they arrived at the hospital. Sophie was happy, certain that she would soon be holding Arthur or Stella. She was about to hug her own baby in her arms. She was going to be a mother. The contractions were two minutes apart and starting to hurt, but they were fine. She could do it, she knew she could. They went up in the lift, and through some security that stopped people stealing babies, and then she was in a room with Rob and a midwife, and the midwife was checking how far on she was.

Sophie was certain that the answer was going to be 'very'. She was going to be one of those people who had a baby so fast that everyone was taken by surprise. There was a woman at yoga who had almost had her son in the hospital lift. That was the sort of birth Sophie was having.

'It's going to be a while yet,' the woman said cheerfully. She was a small woman, with short mousy hair, rosy cheeks and a wide smile. 'Go off and have a walk around if you like.'

'Are you sure?'

'Oh yes. You've got such a lovely taut stomach. Those muscles are going to take a while to let this baby go.'

'Oh,' she said. 'Right. Is it OK if we stick around here?'

'Sure, if you like. If I were you, I'd hit the canteen.'

Sophie was pleased by that.

'She doesn't want me to leave the building,' she told Rob. 'Does she? That means it could happen quickly.'

He laughed at her, in a kind way. 'Babe, it doesn't matter how long this takes. All we have to do is get this baby out into the world in the next few days. OK? And I know you want the water pool and all of that. But if it doesn't happen, it doesn't matter. All right? You and the baby are what matters.'

She looked away. 'I know.'

He took her shoulders and stared at her until she looked up into his face, and giggled.

'You're going to be the best mum ever,' he said, his brown eyes not leaving hers. 'You know that.'

'Mmm.'

'You are. I know we both can't wait to meet Arthur or Stella, but let it take the time it takes. It's started. One thing that is beyond a doubt is the fact that this baby is going to be with us soon. Now, let's go to the canteen like the midwife said, and get a cup of tea and a biscuit. Deal?'

She smiled. 'Deal.'

Six hours after that, she was desperate. Her body was not her own. She was being ripped apart by pain. She longed for it to stop. She gripped Rob's hand and squeezed so hard that she knew she had to be hurting him, but she didn't care. She didn't care about anything. All she wanted was for this to end.

Then the room filled with people. There was talk that she couldn't follow until Marie, the midwife, leaned down right next to her and said, 'We're worried about the baby's heartbeat. It's dropping. We need to get baby out.'

Things were wheeled into the room. A tall man was standing there, and her legs were held up in stirrups, and she couldn't stop making that noise. Rob was not at her side any more, because there were so many other people who needed to be near her.

Then they were wheeling her bed somewhere, and people were running, and they were injecting her and putting up a screen.

When they handed her the creature, she didn't

even know why. It was red and odd-looking, with deep purple patches, and it was wrapped in a blanket.

A woman she didn't know put it into her arms. She took it to be polite, but tried to hand it back soon afterwards.

Rob was crying, somewhere near her head.

'A little boy,' somebody said. 'A beautiful baby boy. You did it.'

She looked around, trying to catch sight of the beautiful baby boy. They had taken him out of her and put him on the table. They must have given her this thing to hold while she was waiting. She supposed they wanted to keep her busy.

'Rob,' she said. 'Take this.'

She passed it to him and noticed him rushing for it, grabbing it carefully before it slipped on to the floor. It was halfway out of the blanket. She tried to get out of bed, but nothing worked. Her legs wouldn't move. She couldn't feel anything below her waist. She started to scream. They were saying things but she just carried on shouting until they put a needle in her.

'Here we are,' said a different woman. 'She's waking up.'

'I need to have my baby,' she said. 'The baby likes music. Where's the music? Where's my birth

27

plan? I need a water birth. With music. Can we start now?'

'Sophie.' A woman with black hair in a bun crouched down beside her. 'Look at me, Sophie. Your baby has been born. We had to do an emergency section. He's here. A little boy. Your partner is holding him. Look. Right there.'

She looked at Rob, suddenly eager for a sight of her baby, but he just had that other thing.

'No, not that,' she said, speaking slowly, to a stupid person. 'Not that. My *baby*. My real baby. That's what I need. It has to be born in water, with the music playing. I'd like to have it now.'

She saw the woman look at someone else, worried. Sophie closed her eyes and pretended to be asleep. Then she really drifted off to sleep. She could hear them talking as she faded away. 'She went through a lot. Maybe when she wakes up . . .' Things like that.

She hoped so. As she sank into blissful sleep, she thought that when she woke up, she would find her baby, and their happy life, the three of them, would be able to start.

Chapter 6

Paris. Walking

I think I am walking the right way for the station. I am so hungry, all of a sudden, that it is hard to know what I am doing. My legs are only working because of my baby. My little boy needs me and my legs are taking me towards him

I tell myself he is with Rob, that Rob will be looking after him. But if I have woken up here with three days lost, anything at all could have happened. Every safety net there has ever been (and we have had fewer than most) has been whipped away. My life has exploded.

I see a side street with lots of little tables outside some restaurants. One of them has the remains of someone's breakfast or lunch on it, and I walk quickly over and grab two pieces of bread from a basket without stopping. There are people sitting drinking coffee, but if they see what I do, they don't say anything.

I eat it quickly as I walk back to the main road. The energy hits me straight away. I will try to do that again.

I catch sight of myself in a shop window and stop for a second. Although I am sure my face looks mad, tear-stained, stressed, confused and is possibly still painted with a thin layer of vomit in places, the rest of me looks strangely good. From the neck down, I have never been so stylish in my life. That is odd.

Somebody put me in these clothes, unless I did it myself. I am wearing my own underwear, I have checked that. I try to imagine myself blacked out. I picture strange hands fastening these clothes around me while I flop around like a rag doll. I try to imagine whose hands they are, and what else that person did to me while I was drugged.

I pick up a whole basket of bread from a table, and walk off with it as fast as I can. I am pretty sure I am heading towards the station. There are signs pointing to it, I think, in this direction.

I eat white bread that is beginning to go crusty where it has been sliced. The crusts are like razors on my lips. I try to make a plan. I push the food in fast until it is all gone, and drop the empty basket into a bin. I need to get back to London, which means I need to catch the train. But I have no money and no passport.

I am not the kind of woman who steals. I am also not the kind of woman who blacks out and wakes up in Paris. How would one steal a passport? Or enough money for a ticket?

I will have to do it somehow. I walk faster. I will call my mum. She owes me money – she always owes me money.

I hate her, but I will call her because I need her. She loves it when things go wrong. This will be the best thing that has happened to her since I've been better.

At the station, which smells like engines and dust and sweat, I walk to a ticket office. I stand in a queue for a while, screwing up my eyes and willing it to go faster, and then I am at the front.

'I need to get the next train to London,' I tell the man, who has a bald head with hair around the sides like a monk. My stomach rumbles loudly. 'I have to get home. To my baby.'

'You must go upstairs, madame,' he says, and points.

Up there, the uniforms are smarter.

'I need to go to London,' I say again, just in case someone might take pity on me. 'I haven't got my passport. Or any money.'

31

'Then you'll have to come back when you have,' says the woman at the ticket office upstairs. She has so much make-up on that I wonder what she really looks like.

'Can't you . . . help me?' I keep talking, quickly. 'I mean, I woke up in Paris and I don't know how I got here and I haven't got anything and . . .'

'If you don't have money, you can get a friend to buy you a ticket online,' she says, and looks over my shoulder for the next person. 'But you will need a passport. Try the embassy.'

I find a cluster of phones in a quiet corner, and pick up a sticky receiver and call the international operator again.

The phone in the flat rings and rings. Again the answerphone does not click on, even though it ought to.

If I am here, on my own, where is Rob? Where is the baby? I think his name is Harry, not Arthur. Where could he be?

If I am in Paris, they could truly be anywhere. What has happened to them? Have they been spirited away? Is Harry with Rob? Is he with someone else?

I was drugged and taken to Paris. Rob was drugged and taken somewhere else. I know this must be true. We were taken away separately, because together we would have been stronger. I bet Rob is somewhere further away than Paris. He is more likely to get his act together, to get himself to the embassy and make sure he is taken home.

Harry is not here. He could be anywhere. The people have come back for him, whoever they were.

I am too scared to find the British Embassy, and their procedures would take too long. I am going to make my own way home.

I call the operator again, wondering whether I am speaking to the same woman each time. This time I give her my mother's number. She is the last person I want to speak to, but the one person I can get to help. She answers straight away. The sound of her voice, from another world but really there, in my ear, makes my legs collapse underneath me. I grab the metal phone and hang on to it to keep me upright. Suddenly I want to be sick again.

'Mum,' I say, and then I cannot say anything. She cannot hear me yet anyway.

'Hello?' She is suspicious, because a strange number, or no number at all, must have shown up on her display.

I listen to the woman doing her thing, asking

whether she will pay for a call from her daughter Sophie in France.

'Oh,' she says. 'Sophie? In France? Are you sure? Oh, go on then.'

'Mum,' I say again.

'What the hell have you gone and done this time?'

I bite my lip. 'I don't know. Look. This is important. You know Roger? Does he still live in Paris?'

'Why are you asking that?'

'Does he, Mum? It's urgent.'

'What the hell are you doing out there?'

'Mum. I need money. I'm here and I don't know why. I've got nothing and I can't get home. I don't know where Rob is. Or Harry. I need to get the train. Could you get Roger to come to the station and bring me some money?'

Roger is my mother's ex-husband. She has three of them, but Roger is her favourite. He is the only one who liked me, and I used to wish he was my dad.

'Can I get Roger to bring you some money?' Her voice is incredulous. 'You call me now, after not even allowing me to see my own grandchild, and ask me to get someone to bring you money?'

'I need to get back. I need to get back to Harry. Roger won't mind. I know that.'

I say Harry's name, hoping that it is right. Mum would love it if I got my baby's name wrong, and I can tell at once that I haven't.

'The grandchild you keep away from me.'

'Please?'

'I haven't got money.'

'Just give me Roger's number. A hundred pounds. That's all. I'll pay him back later today.'

'And then you'll throw me on the scrap heap again.'

'I won't! I won't, I promise.'

'Will you let me see the baby?'

'Yes! If you do this, you can see him.'

'Get him to call me Grandma.'

I take a deep breath.

'All right. He'll call you Grandma.'

There is a long pause, and I know I am going to win when she says, 'So, if he's around, and if he feels inclined to bail you out, where would he find you?'

After a couple more calls, it is decided that lovely Roger will meet me at four o'clock under the huge board that has all the trains listed on it. That seems to me to be the easiest place to meet on this huge busy station. I can hardly believe it, but I have found someone to bail me out. There is a train at thirteen minutes past five. In an ideal world, I will catch it.

Next I think about the passport problem. That is a much harder one to solve. There are hundreds of people around here, and it would be fairly easy to steal one, if I could find someone who looked enough like me. I'm sure they don't look very hard at British passports.

But each of these people would miss their passport straight away. They are about to get on trains. I need to find one somewhere else.

And so, with an hour to go until I am meeting Roger, I set off back on to the streets of Paris, ready to steal a passport.

Chapter 7

London. A year ago

When she looked at it properly, she saw that it was not even human. It was a bad copy of a baby. This creature they had given her was a thing from a fairy tale. It was a deformed alien, a goblin, a monster she could barely look at, let alone look after.

Somehow she had moved now, and she was in a room with three other beds in it, and all of those beds had women in them, and all of those women had babies. They had proper babies. She was the only person with a trick one. One woman was feeding hers, one was sleeping, and the other was sitting up in bed with the baby in her arms, looking at it. That woman looked over at her.

'Hello,' she said.

Sophie said the word in her head, and decided that she should say it back. This was a test of some sort, and she was going to go along with it, for now.

'Hello,' she replied, carefully.

'How are you?' said the woman. She was a bit older than Sophie, with thick hair down to her shoulders and a rosy face. She also looked hugely fat, but Sophie was not sure if that was really true. She probably looked that way herself. People who had just had babies had to be a bit fat.

'I'm *fine*,' she said, trying out a big smile. 'Fine thanks. How about you?'

'Well, it's a bit of a shock, isn't it? But yes. This is amazing. How did it all go?'

She tried to remember her past self, and to say what that woman would have said, if things had happened the way they were meant to happen. There would be someone, Sophie knew, at some point. Someone who would understand. This woman was not that person, and her job here was to say the right thing until she was allowed out of prison.

'It did not go exactly the way I'd planned,' she managed to say. 'How about you?'

'Oh yes. I know. The birth plan went out the window straight away. But, well, we got there.' She smiled at the baby in her arms. 'This is Lily. How about you? Who have you got there?'

The woman nodded towards the little fish tank that was beside Sophie's bed. She had forgotten that the goblin was in there. She looked at it. Its face was less purple and its eyes were closed. It was waiting patiently, biding its time. She was furious to see that it was wearing the white clothes that had been meant for her real baby. She would change it into other clothes as soon as she could.

'Oh,' she said. 'This is . . . Well actually we're still thinking about the name.'

'A little boy? Or a little girl?'

She remembered what they had said when they first gave it to her.

'Boy.'

'Oh, how lovely. If Lily had been a boy we were going to call her Harry. It means "ruler". I like the idea of a baby being born with something to aim for.'

'Harry,' she said. That would do. It was not the name her real baby would have had, if he'd been a boy. This was not Arthur. This one couldn't have the real baby's clothes and it couldn't have the real baby's name. 'Yes. Harry. That's its name.'

'Oh, how funny!' The woman looked pleased. 'Good choice!'

The goblin kept sleeping. Sophie closed her eyes.

When Rob arrived, she looked at him hard, trying to work out whose side he was on. This was important. If he was with her, then they would work it out together. There were things they would need to do before they would be allowed the real baby. There would be tasks. This was all a test.

If Rob was on the other side, the side that pretended this was Arthur, then she would have to do it alone.

He was suddenly standing there and smiling at her, but his eyes weren't smiling at all. He put a bag of things down on the end of the bed, and a paper cup from a coffee shop on the little table. When he sat on the bed, the whole mattress sloped down. Rob was much bigger than most people.

'How are you doing?' he said. 'Are you feeling any better, Sophie?'

She nodded. Now was not the time to talk properly.

'Much better, thanks,' she said, and she remembered to smile.

He kissed her on the cheek. 'That's wonderful news,' he said. 'Look, I got you a coffee because I'm sure whatever they serve here won't meet your standards. And there's some croissants and things in the bag, and chocolate and, you know, all that. When you come home, we'll get some bubbly and, you know, proper drinks. You've really been through it. That was not the way we'd planned it, was it? Oh, I'm so glad you're better. You scared me by freaking out like that.'

He was talking and talking and not waiting for her to say anything back. She was glad.

'I mean, so much for the birth plan. I can't believe we thought we could take control of a process like that. I was so scared, my darling. So very, very scared for you. I thought I was going to lose you. Both of you. You probably weren't aware of it at the time, but even the doctors got worried about you. I could see it. You poor thing – no wonder you freaked out. You just rest and get yourself back on your feet. So, has he been feeding?'

He walked around to the tank, and stared at the thing. She watched his face, waiting for the disgust and confusion to show.

'I haven't fed him for a while,' she said carefully. In fact she was pretty sure she hadn't fed it at all. 'He's just been asleep. I haven't been awake very long.'

'That's fine. I'm sure he'll let you know when he wants something.'

He was leaning over, staring at the creature. He was hiding his real feelings very well indeed.

'Hey there, Arthur,' he said, and Sophie's blood turned to ice. 'Hey, little boy. You're my son. I'm your dad. We're going to do amazing things together, us three. Welcome to the world!'

'It's not Arthur,' she said quickly. '*He's* not Arthur, I mean. He's Harry.'

Rob frowned up at her. 'But we said if we had a boy he'd be Arthur. We both loved that name. It was agreed from the start. Arthur and Stella!'

He was hurt. She smiled and made her face as blank as she could. It was, she knew, the only way she was going to get through this.

'I know we did,' she said. 'But look at him. This is Harry. It's not Arthur, is it?'

Rob stared at her, and then stared at the goblin. He sighed.

'If you say so,' he said. 'After all that, I can hardly argue. Could it be Harry Arthur? A bit of a mouthful, but that would be all right, wouldn't it?'

She shook her head. 'Let's save Arthur for the next one.'

He paused. 'Or we could make a final decision later.'

She shrugged, as if she didn't care. 'OK. But this baby is Harry. All right?' She remembered what the woman opposite had said. 'It means "ruler".'

'Fine.'

He was disappointed. Arthur had been his grandfather's name, and he had insisted on it for their son, right from the start. Even before he met her, when he had been single and longed for a baby, his first son was going to be Arthur. The fact that he was letting her change it to a random name that came from the woman in the opposite bed made her wonder if he knew this was the wrong baby too. The real baby, when they found him, was going to be Arthur. This one could have any old name. It could have the second-hand name she'd found at the hospital.

The thing she had been dreading happened. The creature started wriggling and sniffing and whimpering. Its arms started pumping around, and its face screwed up. Rob leaned down and picked it up at once.

'Here you go,' he said. 'Hey, Harry. Little Harry. We'll get used to that. You come to Daddy.'

She stared at him. He really didn't know.

Chapter 8

Stealing in Paris

I need to go to where the tourists are. That is where I will find a white woman of about my age, with a passport in her handbag. She is out there.

I close my eyes and try to work out where to find her.

'Where,' I ask a man in uniform, 'do the tourists go near here?'

He stops, stares into my eyes and then laughs loudly.

'Little time before train?' he asks. I nod, pleased with this idea, and he directs me to a church that I think he says is on the top of a hill nearby.

Twenty minutes later, I am sweating and breathless, at the top of a hill. And there it is, handed to me by a world that is finally on my side. In the crowd of tourists standing by a wall and staring out at the view of the city is a white woman with brown hair, her bag gaping open. I stand behind her. Her passport is right there.

She is talking to a man next to her, laughing and waving an arm.

'Last time it was raining,' she is saying, and she sounds British.

There are lots of people around. She should not stand here with her bag wide open. This almost serves her right, though I am so grateful to her that I cannot quite think that.

An old man brushes past me. I take a step forward so I am right up against this woman, with her blue shorts stretched across her broad hips.

I reach in, as slowly and carefully as I can, and take the passport in my fingertips. Her purse snags on it as I lift it up, and for a moment I think she is going to turn around and catch me, but the purse drops back and I have it, free of the bag, in my hand.

I turn and melt away into the crowd. I am down the steps, away from the church with its huge domes, and running as fast as I can back towards the station. My legs take me down the right roads, and then I am there.

My heart pounds as I run back to the huge

station. I cannot believe I did that and that no one, so far, has caught up with me. I expect to be arrested at any moment. I stay in the crowds as much as I can, walking around the busy parts of the station, not even daring to look at the passport. In the end I go down to the underground level and find a loo, which is grimy and smelly, and lock myself in a stall. I put the lid down, sit on it, and open the passport with trembling hands.

It is, indeed, a British passport, and it belongs to a woman called Hazel Trent. She is eight years older than I am. If anyone looks closely they will see at once that I am not her, but if they don't, I might get away with it. This is the only plan I've got.

It is nearly four o'clock. I stand under the huge board that is clicking away as the place-names and times change. There are armed police everywhere I look, but none of them seem interested in anything that is going on. A woman comes up to me begging, but I shake my head.

'Wrong person,' I say, and she moves on at once.

Four o'clock comes and goes. If Roger doesn't show up, then Hazel Trent's passport will be no use to me at all. Five past four arrives and

I am wondering whether I can steal money, and how to do that without being instantly arrested by one of the armed police. At ten past four, as I am frantic with worry, he is suddenly in front of me.

'Sophie Mayes,' he says, and he makes a little bow.

I haven't seen Roger for nearly ten years. He used to be a proper working-class Londoner, but now he looks like a man who has lived in Paris all his life. He is wearing a smart shirt and a pair of cream trousers, and he has grown a little grey moustache.

'Roger.' I fall on him, sobbing into his shoulder.

'I believe you are in need of funds,' he says, and I wonder what he ever saw in my mother. He takes out an envelope and hands it to me. As I am about to tell him everything, he kisses my cheek and slips away.

Chapter 9

London. A year ago

If she pretended to be a goblin mother, she could trick them all into thinking she hadn't realised. She needed to get the boxes ticked so she would be allowed to go home. All the hospital staff wanted her to go home, because they had lots to do and it was much easier for them if she was better. They were on the side of a woman who was doing things right.

In Sophie's mind she became a goblin lady, deformed and ugly. She looked at the baby goblin with a goblin mummy's eyes and managed to pretend she thought it was beautiful. She was careful to smile all the time and to say 'Fine, thanks!' in a bright voice.

They let her go home.

As soon as they got into the flat, the three of them, Sophie started to search. This was the place to look for Arthur. It was, after all, his home, full of his things. That was his bedroom, and this was his crib. There were drawers filled with his clothes, and everything was ready for him.

'What are you doing?' asked Rob, as she opened cupboards and checked every baby-sized space they had.

'Looking,' she said, vaguely.

'What for?'

'Oh. You know. Checking it all.'

The pretend baby was in its car seat. That was the seat they had bought for Arthur. Sophie did not blame anyone for what had happened. She knew it was her fault that it had all gone wrong. Something had happened to stop him being born properly, and this other creature had arrived instead. It probably happened all the time. It wasn't in the books because it was a thing you had to work out and deal with yourself. It was a trial.

'Let's have a photo,' said Rob, and she picked up the creature from its car seat, and held it the way she knew she was supposed to hold it, with its head into the crook of her elbow. She closed her eyes for a second and pretended to be the goblin mum, and she smiled. The photo was taken, and they looked at it together.

'You look different,' Rob said, and he stared into her eyes for a second.

'I am different.' It was as close as she dared get to talking about it.

'Why are you crying?'

She blinked and sniffed and said she didn't know. That seemed to be the right answer. Rob hugged her and she sobbed into his bulky shoulder.

The nights were difficult. It kept waking up. She did everything she was supposed to do, and nobody expected much of her. If the goblin was wearing (Arthur's) clothes, and if it drank milk from the bottles she had made Rob buy, against his will, and if it was often asleep, everyone said she was doing a wonderful job. They saw what they wanted to see.

Only Rob knew that she had noticed she had the wrong baby. She never told him, but she would watch him looking at her, and it was as if he were a stranger. He would stare at her, seeing through everything, and then he would turn away.

Rob had to go back to work in the end. Because he was a teacher, and because it was summer, he stayed at home longer than most fathers would, but then it was September, and her world, the nightmare world that she was only just holding together as it was, fell apart completely.

He called Sophie's friend, Jess, the week before

term started, when he thought Sophie wasn't listening. He took his phone into the bathroom and locked the door, and she stood outside and listened to every word, because she had known that he was up to something.

'Could you come over?' he said. 'Could you keep an eye on her? She's not right and I've got no idea what to do. I don't like leaving her, Jess.'

From his replies, Sophie could tell that Jess was agreeing. Even though her younger girl, Rose, was starting school and Jess was about to have her first free time for ages, she was going to come and babysit Sophie and her alien goblin baby.

Later that day, the phone rang.

'Sophie,' said Jess. 'How are you? Could I come over on Monday? It would be so lovely to spend some time with you and Harry, and with Rob back at school I'm sure you could do with some company. Is that OK? I'll bring food.'

Sophie managed not to laugh. 'OK,' she said.

On Monday she had a shower and dressed herself in a loose skirt (one of the few things that fitted her) and a nice top. She washed her hair and dried it with a hairdryer. She put on a tiny bit of make-up, but didn't recognise herself, so took it off again.

Then she stood over the cot and stared at the thing.

Every time she looked, she wanted it to have changed into Arthur. Whoever had swapped them the first time would have to change them back one day. She hoped they would, anyway. She screwed her eyes tight shut and pictured her real baby lying there. The baby she had imagined would have soft rosy cheeks, and its hair would be light, and it would not be a creature from a different planet. It would be hers.

She opened her eyes, longing for Arthur.

It was still Harry.

The doorbell rang.

'Hi!' said Jess, smiling. She was standing in the rain. Her hair was long and dyed black and dripping, and she was holding two bags of stuff. 'Right. I'm here to help. Is he sleeping?'

Sophie stood back to let her in. She didn't care if he was sleeping or not. As she closed the door behind Jess, she noticed a sound but wasn't sure what it was. Then she realised that Jess was staring at her.

'Sophie?' she said. 'Aren't you going to pick him up?'

It was the goblin crying. She hadn't noticed. Normally Rob would pick him up and bring him to her.

'Oh yes,' she said. 'I'd better.'

Jess stayed all day. She called her husband, Peter, to arrange for the girls to be collected from school. She talked about any old thing, made the creature its bottles, and put food in front of Sophie far more often than she wanted to eat.

'My friend Lauren,' she said, 'she's just discovered she can't carry a baby to term. It's hellish for her.'

Sophie knew what Jess meant. She meant that she, Sophie, should be grateful that she had a baby at all. She ignored that.

'I'm sure she'll be fine,' she said, in a neutral voice.

As the days went on, it got worse. Jess couldn't be there all day, every day, and when Sophie was alone, she tried so hard to do the things she was meant to do that she got them wrong. She didn't pick the creature up. She picked him up when he was sleeping and made him cry. She knew that she sometimes forgot to feed him. She was finding it harder and harder to be the goblin mother.

When Rob came home, he stared at her, and sent texts on his phone which, when she went to look at them, had been deleted. She knew she was getting it all wrong. She was failing the tests. She was never going to get her Arthur. She wondered if she was meant to jump off a bridge

with the creature in her arms. She started plan-
ning it.

Before she could do it, everything changed.

The creature that was meant to be her baby
was cold. It was cold because she had forgotten
that it was autumn now, and she had dressed it
just in a vest and nappy, and put it in a pushchair
in the courtyard for some fresh air. When she
realised it was too cold, because it was crying so
loudly a neighbour came over, she brought it in
and warmed it up by lying it down on the sofa
with a pile of blankets on top of it, and the heating
turned up high. Then it was too hot.

She had no idea what to do. So she thought
she'd better cool it down again quickly, or they
would think she wasn't looking after it and would
never give her real baby back. The quickest way
to cool something down, she supposed, would be
to put it in the fridge.

She picked it up and carried it, as carefully as a
goblin mother would have done, to the tall fridge in
the corner of the kitchen. There were vegetables
in the drawer at the bottom, but if she took them
out, that would be the right-sized place for a baby
to lie until it was cool. She opened the fridge door
and, holding the baby in one arm, pulled out all
the vegetables and threw them on to the floor. It

fitted into the plastic drawer exactly, and one single lettuce leaf was left behind, soft under its head. The baby looked at her and its face crumpled as she closed the door.

She would have to remember to go and get it out again quite soon.

Sophie decided to set the oven timer to remind herself. Two minutes should do it.

When the beeper went off, she was in the sitting room, trying to remember what it was she was not allowed to forget.

Chapter 10

Leaving Paris

I make myself sit still on the train. I lean back and try to be natural, staring out of the window and doing my best to look like everyone else. I wish I had a book, because then I could stare at it, or actually read it and forget my real life for a while.

I bite my lip and clench my fists and hope against hope that poor Hazel Trent is not missing her passport. How, I wonder, does that work? If she reported it missing, would anyone notice it being used for travel at that very moment? As long as I get through security at St Pancras, and back to Harry, then I don't care what they do to me.

When the train starts moving, at exactly 17.13, a tiny part of me relaxes. I am moving, slowly and then faster, in the direction of Harry and Rob. I hope I am. If they are in London, I am going the right way.

I look out of the window, wondering whether I saw this landscape when I was on my way here. I might have done, but I have no memory at all. I try, again, to remember the last thing that happened. I scour my mind for any clues at all.

It was Sunday night, and now it is Thursday. On Sunday night I put Harry to bed as I always do. He stood up in his cot and watched me leave the room, and I went back twice to kiss him and to try to lie him down. He giggled and got up again. I kissed his hair, his soft curly hair, and stroked his cheek, and he tried to grab me to stop me leaving the room.

I walked out and closed the door, and he chattered to himself for a bit and curled up to sleep.

Rob was washing up in the kitchen. As it was (it still is, I suppose) the school holidays, he was around and was doing most of the cooking and a lot of the housework. Rob is not one of those men who expects to be waited on, though when it's term time and he is working fourteen-hour days, I cook and do all the house stuff.

I remember walking up behind him and nuzzling into his neck. He stopped and turned around and looked at me for a long time.

'Sophie,' he said. He gazed at me for so long that I started to laugh.

'What?'

'Oh, nothing. It's just, you know. Still good to have you back.'

'Don't.'

'Sorry. Have a drink? Glass of wine?'

'If you insist.'

'A summer evening? Our child sleeping peacefully? My Sophie back? Everything as it should be? I insist. I know you don't like being reminded of it, but still, you have done an amazing thing.'

I hugged him. I could not speak. I knew I would carry the guilt with me for ever.

We spent a happy, normal evening together. I went to bed after Rob, because I stayed up finishing the book I was reading. He was fast asleep by the time I got to bed, and I lay next to him and held him and thought how incredibly lucky I was to have him. Everything was going to be all right.

'Let's have another baby.' I whispered that. I hadn't expected him to hear me, but he turned over.

'You think you could do that?' he asked softly.

'Yes.'

And that is the last thing I remember.

The towns and fields and villages and farms outside the window are not very interesting. There is a cloudy, slate-coloured sky, and everything looks dull and flat. I look at the people inside the train instead, and wonder what they are all doing. I want to know what they are like. I try to focus on them, on anything other than myself and the terrible fact that I have lost my child.

I have lost him. The world has taken him from me.

'But I love him,' I say, and because the man opposite looks up at me sharply, I realise I have said it out loud. I did not mean to do that. The world does not understand how much I adore him. This has happened to remind me that I do not deserve him.

I try to read a safety card, desperate for something to think about. I stare at towns rushing past the window, trying to notice the way everything is slightly different from the way it is at home. The road signs are different. The roads are empty. The houses are not at all the same.

Although I don't want to, I search inside myself, looking for guilt. There is plenty of it there. However, it is old. It stops nine months ago. There is nothing recent. Nothing at all.

I go to the train loo and stare at myself in the mirror. I do not look exactly like myself. That is not Sophie Mayes. It is a woman who looks a bit like Sophie Mayes. My hair is ratty and messy, and I push it down with my hands and try to make it chic. My odd green clothes make me look different, and I am slightly thinner than I used to be. Perhaps I didn't eat between Sunday and today. I haven't eaten much today, and that is why I feel so dizzy.

It is amazing how many things you cannot do without money.

The train glides into a tunnel, and I realise it must be the tunnel that comes out in England. I stare at the woman in the mirror for a bit longer, and set off down the train, trying to breathe, trying not to think.

Chapter 11

London. 11 months ago

Someone was banging on the door. She ignored it. The oven timer was still beeping. She had broken the rules, she knew she had, but she was not quite sure which rules, or what she had done.

The banging stopped, but then it started again, this time on the window. The trouble with living in a ground-floor flat was that if you were hiding in the sitting room pretending to be out, the person on the doorstep could easily see you if they tried.

'Sophie!' Jess shouted.

Sophie looked at her. She was staring through the window now, her hands to the glass, her hair around her head like a bright black halo.

'Coming,' Sophie said, and went to the front door and let her in. She always did what Jess told her to do.

As soon as she came through the door of the flat, rather than the one that led to the whole house, Jess took Sophie by the shoulders.

'Are you OK? Where's Harry?'

Sophie bit her lip. That was the thing – that was what she had done wrong.

'He was hot,' she said. She could not say anything more. She knew she had done something terrible and horrible. She had broken all the rules and now they would not let her have any baby at all. She would not be allowed her real baby, or even the goblin.

Suddenly she wanted the goblin. They would never let her have the baby she had wanted. Harry would do.

Harry, she thought, was her baby. She hadn't noticed it happening, but he had changed back. They had swapped him. He was her own darling baby, and she needed him. She had tried to cool him down.

'He was hot? Where is he?'

Sophie could not say it. She pointed and let Jess find him herself. She stood still and listened.

'He was hot?' Jess was talking to Sophie, but muttering to herself. 'Did you put him outside? Did you put him in a cold bath? He's not in the bath, is he? Oh Sophie!'

Jess followed Sophie's gaze, and ran to the corner of the kitchen.

Sophie heard her gasp. She heard the door

seal peel open, and she heard the drawer being pulled out, and she heard her find him. The baby started to cry. Jess was taking huge deep breaths and holding him tight and running for the phone.

The flat was filled with people. There was an ambulance for the baby, and another one for Sophie. She was kept away from him. His ambulance went to the hospital. Hers went to a different sort of hospital. She did not see Rob. He went to Harry.

Sophie was in a hospital bed and she swallowed a lot of pills, and she lay back and closed her eyes and went to sleep. The feelings, the real feelings, had been starting to come back, but the pills made her feel nothing at all.

Chapter 12

London. Now

I am the first off the train and I run through security. I have discarded the idea that I could be arrested for stealing Hazel Trent's passport. That is not even an issue. I wave it at an immigration man who doesn't even open it. I could have taken anyone's identity. That could have been an old man's passport. I did not need to choose her so carefully.

The ticket lets me through the barriers. Of course it does. I am no longer Hazel. I am myself, and I am home. Free. In London. I am more terrified than I have ever been in my life.

St Pancras station is huge and shiny, filled with expensive shops. Someone is playing the piano. There are people around, and the lighting has been stylishly planned, and I hate the place, hate it, hate it, because I can't find the way out. I run past the piano, then double back and put the passport down on it, saying a silent thank-you to Hazel Trent, hoping she gets a new passport easily and that her insurance pays for it all.

Then I am standing at the top of the stairs to the Tube station, and I don't know what to do. I need help. I need someone who will help me find Rob and Harry. I cannot do this on my own.

Jess lives nearby, up by the Caledonian Road. I will go to her. I will run all the way, because I don't have any luggage, and I will bang on her door and make her help me.

I set off up the road, running as fast as I can.

Jess opens the door and stares. I look at her, my best friend, her hair now short and dyed bright red. As soon as I see her, I want to cry, but I force myself not to. I have held it together for all this time, I can do it for a few minutes longer. My legs go weak and I reach out to steady myself on the nearest wall.

'Sophie,' she says, and she looks wary.

I start talking at once.

'Jess,' I say. 'You have to help me. Terrible things have happened. Awful ones. I don't know what's happened to Rob and Harry. They've gone.'

She takes a hand and leads me into the house. 'Gone?'

'Yes. Gone. I just – I woke up, Jess, and I was in Paris, and I've got no idea . . .'

'Oh Sophie. Those are new clothes, aren't they? You look terrible. You went to *Paris*? Seriously?'

She leads me into the kitchen and sits me down at the table. I see the way she is looking at me and I want to cry.

'I didn't *go* there. But I *was* there. But it's Rob and Harry. They've been taken somewhere too. They're not at home.'

'Are you sure, Sophie? Really?'

'Yes.'

'How do you know?'

'They didn't answer the phone.'

'And that means . . .?'

I am suddenly furious. Jess hands me a cup of tea that I haven't noticed her making. I hold it and bite my lip.

'Look. I went to sleep, Jess, on Sunday night at home as normal. And then I woke up on Thursday, in a room I'd never seen before, in Paris. I didn't do that! Someone did it to me. And every time I managed to call home, they didn't answer.'

She stares at me for a long time.

'I'll try them,' she says in the end, and she takes her phone out of her pocket and presses some buttons.

I hear Rob answer after three rings.

'Jess,' he says. 'Have you seen Sophie?'

'She's right here,' she says, looking at me and edging backwards a little. 'In my kitchen. She says she woke up . . .' she sounds nervous, 'in Paris.'

I have no idea what is going on. I hear Jess making hushed plans with my partner, but I tune out of what they are. I must be mad, I think. It must be me. All along, all of that. It was me.

'Come on,' she says. 'I'm taking you home.'

On the Tube, I realise I have forgotten where I am, in hours and in days.

'Is it still Thursday?' I ask.

She looks at me sharply, then smiles.

'Yes, Sophie,' she says. 'It's still Thursday. It's about seven, I think. How on earth did you get yourself back from Paris and to my front door?'

'Oh. I was so scared about Harry that I just did.'

I feel a little uneasy about that. I travelled as Hazel Trent and left her passport on top of the piano at St Pancras. That will surely come back to haunt me. 'I got my mum to arrange some money,' I add. 'You remember her ex? Roger?'

'Your *mum*?'

'I had to promise to let her see Harry. And she got Roger to bring me some cash.'

'You're going to let your mum see Harry? Sophie . . .'

'I know. I won't really. I just needed money. Desperately. I had to get home. I had to start looking for him, because how can I know what they've actually done with him? With my baby? If I was taken somewhere, he was too, and . . .' I hear my voice tailing off. This does not sound convincing, because I heard Jess talking to Rob on the phone half an hour ago. 'I don't know,' I end, lamely.

'Soph,' says Jess, and she takes my hand and I can see that she is trying to be very kind indeed. 'Soph, this is not some terrible conspiracy. Nobody spirited you to Paris in your sleep. How on earth would they have done that? You did it, didn't you? You did it yourself. It's not as if . . .'

I take a deep breath.

'I know.'

It is not as if I have a clean record. It is not as if I have never done anything that made no sense. A woman who once put her baby in the veg drawer of the fridge to cool down is a woman who would black out and find herself in a strange room, wearing strange clothes, in

Paris. Other women would not do that. I would. Perhaps I did. I don't think so, but nobody else would have done it.

'You know your problems have been coming back,' Jess says quietly. 'You know they have. If you've been away since Sunday and you haven't got anything with you, then you've definitely stopped the pills.'

I cling on to her hand, trying to hold myself together.

'You've been acting strangely for a while, you know. I didn't mention it, but a few times you've arranged to meet me and then not turned up, and when I've called you've had no idea. Remember when you texted to ask me over? And when we arrived you weren't expecting us. But you'd sent the text – it was on your phone. Those kinds of things. Look. It's OK, darling. We'll get you home. Back to the right people. You can get fixed again.'

I had no idea I needed to get fixed again.

Rob opens the door, smiling. His face is open and I can see the nervous relief all over his face.

'Hey, Soph!' He steps forward and hugs me, and it is only then that I feel the tension. 'You're back. Everything OK?'

I stare at him. 'What?'

'You took off saying you were going to clear your head. Are you feeling better?'

I cannot answer. I walk in through the front door and try to work out what on earth is happening.

'Where's Harry?' I demand.

'He's in there,' says Rob. 'Just playing a bit before bed.'

I walk towards the sitting room, knowing that I am going to see something terrible. Harry will be gone. He will be the goblin I used to see. It will be a different baby, a dog, a kitten. There will be blood all over the room. He will be dead. All of that flashes through my mind as I take the five steps.

He is sitting on the floor, wearing his pyjamas and playing with his wooden building blocks. As I walk in, he turns around and laughs.

'Mama,' he says, and he puts the block carefully down, turns around and crawls to me. He sits at my feet and lifts his arms, asking to be picked up.

I reach down and take him. He sits on my hip and reaches for my hair, holding it for comfort as he always does.

I hold him close. I smell him.

The thing that just happened to me, whatever it was, is over.

Chapter 13

London. Nine months ago

They kept her on a ward with other crazy women, and she got better quickly. They fed her all kinds of pills, and she could feel them deadening her inside and making her world flat and strange, but she took them because she needed the doctors to let her back to her baby.

Rob brought him to visit her, and she clung to him and cried. She smelled his hair and wondered how much damage she had done to him. He was Arthur and he was Harry. Secretly she still believed they had swapped him for a while, but she knew that she would never say that aloud to anyone, ever. He was hers now – he was Harry, and yet he was the baby she wanted. Everything had shifted slightly and fallen into its place.

Rob was looking after him at home. Jess was helping, and so were other people. There was a friend of Jess's, and there were people from work, people she knew and people she didn't know. People were 'rallying round', he said.

Sophie was doing well. When they told her that, she wanted to laugh, but not because it was funny. She had been *going* to do it all well, but she had ended up being worse than her own mother, who had slipped in to stand at her bedside and sneer.

'Well,' she said. 'You thought it would be a piece of piss. But it wasn't, was it? You've messed it up worse than anyone I've ever known. I hope they take him away from you and you never see him again. Poor little bugger.'

She turned her face away and closed her eyes until her mother left, still clutching the horrible flowers she had brought with her. Sophie's mother had never wanted a child, had never bonded with her, and had blamed Sophie for her father leaving. Looking back now, Sophie supposed her mother had been depressed, and could have done with some pills herself. However, she was never going to find it in her heart to feel sorry for her.

Sophie got better, and Rob came with Harry every day, and when she had gazed at her baby, and stroked him, and said sorry to him again and again and again, she looked at Rob. She could see that he had changed. Her weirdness scared him and he didn't love her any more. It showed clearly on his face. He chatted away and tried to say the right things, but his eyes avoided hers and his face was like a mask.

When they got home, he tried to pretend things were normal. They both did. Sophie rushed around doing things. She looked after Harry even though it took her ages to find where his stuff was, because Rob had moved everything around. She made dinner, tidied the house, fed the baby and tried to make up for it all. She went to her appointments and took her pills, even though she was sure she no longer needed them.

In the end, Rob went back to work. When she was cleaning one day, she found a bag at the back of a cupboard, and it was packed with clothes for Rob and for Harry, with a spare toothbrush, and nappies, and everything they could possibly need.

There was nothing of hers in there.

It chilled her. She pushed it back and never said she had seen it. Every now and then she would go back and check, and as Harry grew, the clothes in it were swapped for bigger ones.

Rob was preparing to run away, with her baby, if she went mad again. But that, she swore to herself, was never going to happen.

Chapter 14

London. Now

I settle nervously back into normal life. I accept that I must have lost all reason and all control and gone to Paris, somehow, on my own. I bought new clothes and lost my passport and money, and found my way into that room and lay down on the bed. I have no idea how I could possibly have done that, but I have no other ideas.

It is terrifying, and Rob keeps asking me more about it.

'You must remember *something*,' he says, and I shake my head and ask him to stop.

'I can't talk about it,' I tell him. 'Please.'

He shrugs and walks away. He says I told him I was going, on Monday morning. He says I packed a bag and set off for the Tube. It must have happened. There is no other option.

Every morning my heart pounds for the

seconds between waking up and checking that I am in the right bed. I open my eyes wide and look around. I see our walls and our furniture, crammed into the little room. I reach an arm down and touch the floor, and there it is, the floor, with its carpet, not with floorboards. I check that I am not about to be sick, that there are not red and white curtains fluttering in the breeze, that the sounds and smells are not of Paris but of home.

And it is only when I have checked all of that that I can run to my baby boy.

A day goes by, and another, and things are normal. I check the house, looking for clues as to what was going on in my head, but I find nothing. I have not written anything down, have not hidden anything away. None of my friends knows anything about it. According to my bank account, I did not buy a ticket to Paris. I did not, apparently, buy anything when I got there. Nothing has come out of my bank account. I am going mad.

And my passport is in the drawer, in its place.

Rob and Harry's running-away bag is no longer at the back of the cupboard. I have no idea what that means.

On the third day, the buzzer buzzes. Rob is

out with Harry, 'so you can rest', he said, even though I didn't want to rest. He is treating me like an invalid, treading too carefully around me.

I answer without saying anything, because I am distracted by a cup of coffee I am in the middle of making.

'Let me in, then!' says a woman's voice. I press the button without a word.

When she reaches our door, I am waiting for her. She is about my age, with dyed blond hair loose over her shoulders, and she is wearing a denim jacket and a denim skirt. She looks as if she spends a lot of time on her appearance, but all the same, I would never do double denim.

She stares at me and I stare back. I have seen this woman before. The sight of her rings huge alarm bells, but I cannot think why. Perhaps I saw her in Paris, in my lost days.

'Hello?' I say, and I take half a step forward.

'Oh,' she says. 'Sorry. Wrong flat.'

'Who are you looking for?'

She pauses long enough for me to know she is lying.

'Sarah,' she says. 'I thought you were Sarah. Sorry.'

'Rob's out,' I say. I don't know why I say it, but I am sure she has come for Rob.

'Oh. Um. Who's Rob?'

'Don't worry.'

'Sorry to have bothered you.'

She practically runs back out to the street. Without even thinking about it, I call Rob's phone. If I can make her call go to voicemail, maybe she will leave a message. I can access our voicemails from the landline, because I set that up when I was ill. I used to log into Rob's voicemails to see if he was getting messages from the evil overlords who had my real baby. I shudder at the thought.

Everything about that woman has put my senses on high alert. She spells danger.

He answers the phone. 'Everything OK, Soph?'

'Oh, fine,' I tell him, and I say any old thing to keep his phone busy. 'I think I remembered some stuff about my trip to Paris,' I pretend.

'No way! What do you remember?'

I talk off the top of my head. 'I think I went there in a car,' I tell him. 'I remember looking out of the window. And I remember going into a shop and buying clothes. Those ones, I mean, the ones I was wearing. But also some others. Something yellow, I think, because I thought that would be nice in the summer. That's funny, isn't it, since I never really care about clothes?'

'Yes. Yes, it *is* funny. Do you remember how you got to that room?'

'No. No, not yet. But maybe I will. How's Harry? Are you two OK?'

'Of course we are. We're heading to the play park. You get some rest, all right? Rest up.'

He is always saying that. I don't want to rest, but that doesn't seem to make a difference. We chat for a while longer, and when I can tell he wants me off the phone, I hang up.

Immediately I dial his voicemail number and enter the code.

'You have one new message,' says the electronic lady. 'To listen to your messages, press one.'

My finger shakes as I press one. As she starts to speak, I sink down to the floor. I close my eyes. I bite my lip. I try very, very hard not to hurl the phone across the room and scream.

What she says changes everything. And I know where I have seen her before.

Chapter 15

London. Six months ago

Sophie had taken the baby out to the play park even though it looked like rain. She filled each day with things to do, with fun. She did not want Harry bored at home for one moment.

There was only one other child at the swings. It was a girl, older than Harry, and she was running up the steps of the slide and throwing herself down fearlessly, over and over again. Sophie stared at her and tried to imagine Harry walking, then running, climbing and going where he wanted to go, rather than where she put him. It was a thought that made her smile.

Harry could only just sit up. He was six months old, and for three months, since she got better, Sophie had been trying to make up for his terrible start in life. She had been the best mother she could be, every moment of every day, but it could never be enough.

She propped him in the swing. He barely bent at the waist in his snowsuit, and she had to wedge a blanket behind him to keep him from slumping sideways.

He turned and looked at her, his dark blue eyes gleaming, his mouth smiling so hard it changed the shape of his face.

'Here you go, darling,' she said, and even though it was raining, she didn't care. He was wrapped up against the weather, and she deserved to get wet. 'Let's give you a push.'

It was heavy inside her, the way she had failed him. She tried to make up for it every day. She held him close, sniffed his hair, stroked his cheek. He, in turn, became a happy baby, looking for her all the time, smiling when he saw her.

Sophie was her old self again, though in a world that was made flat and predictable by the pills she took. Even that, however, could not stop her loving Harry with a passion she had never imagined before. She adored him. Everything she had felt about him before baffled her. It was not her having those feelings. They were not about him. She tried to take herself back into that mindset, but it didn't work. She had been someone else. They talked about imbalances in the brain, and that made sense. It was just something slightly wrong that had needed fixing, and now it was fixed.

It was raining harder. Harry chuckled every time the swing changed direction, but she was going to have to get him in the pushchair with the rain cover over him soon, or she would feel like a bad mother. She could never bear to do anything that made her look like a bad mother.

They would leave the park and, she suddenly decided, catch a bus. A few stops on a double-decker would take them close to Rob's school, and they could go to a café and text him to see if he had any time between lessons to pop out and say hello. Harry would like the bus, if they sat upstairs. Babies liked big red buses. Their wheels went round and round.

She knew that Harry was, in fact, far too little to enjoy being on a bus, but she did it anyway. The rain splattered on to the window and they both stared at the drops as they coursed down the glass.

The café was busy, mainly with women with babies, like her, though they were mostly in chatty groups. Sophie found a high chair for Harry and folded the pushchair into a corner.

She took Harry to the loos to change his nappy, because she could smell that it needed doing. He lay on the flimsy pull-down changing table and held his feet and giggled, while she got a clean nappy on him quickly. She was good at that kind of thing now.

When they came out, two people at a corner table caught her eye. They were a woman with bright blond hair, red lipstick and a belted raincoat, and a man with his back to Sophie. They were leaning towards each other, whispering.

Sophie walked up to the counter, Harry under her arm facing out, the way he liked it at the moment. She stood with her back to the couple, her heart pounding so hard that she was surprised the cups weren't falling off their shelves.

There might as well have been no one else in the room but her, Harry and the couple. That man was Rob. She had not seen his face, but she was certain of it. He was wearing Rob's jumper. He had Rob's hair. There had been a leather 'man bag' on the floor by his feet, and that belonged to Rob. They used to laugh about it. Rob said it wasn't fair that only women got to carry things around in nice bags. This was the café near his school. Sophie had never seen the woman before in her life. She tried to tell herself that it must just be another teacher, that she and Rob were here on work business, but she could see instantly that it was more than that.

'A large coffee, please,' she said quietly, casting

around for something else to order to keep her away from Rob for a few seconds more. 'And one of those cookies. Thanks!'

The door banged but she didn't look round. She paid for the things, waited for the coffee, delaying the moment when she had to see for certain that it was him, that he was here, without her, with a woman.

When, eventually, she went to put Harry in the chair so she could carry the coffee safely, the table was empty. Rob and the woman were gone. It was as if they had never been there.

She asked him about it later, of course.

'Were you at the café near your school today?' Her voice was bright, cheerful. She wanted him to say 'Yes, I had a meeting there about the school trip.' Anything would have done.

'Not a moment to get out. No. Why?'

'Oh. I thought I saw you in there. But maybe it wasn't you.'

'Not maybe.' He smiled. 'It wasn't me. If you'd seen me, we'd probably have said hello, don't you think? It's nice, though, if you think you see me in places. That's what people do, isn't it, when they're in love?'

She nodded, and tried to look normal.

'Yes,' she said. 'I suppose it is.'

Chapter 16

London. Now

'Rob, what the hell?' the woman's message said. 'I went to the flat but she was there! I thought I was picking stuff up? I had my car outside, double-parked. Call me. Where the hell are you two anyway? I didn't go through that whole farce just for you to back out on me now! That was your idea, and it was a stupid one.'

The words play in my head, over and over again. *I didn't go through that whole farce just for you to back out on me now. That was your idea.*

I want to be sick. Instead, I've got things to do. I pour myself a glass of wine and start searching every inch of the flat. I cannot put my finger on what is going on, but I know that it is something very, very bad.

He took me to France, and she came too. That is all that can mean. They drugged me and took me there and put me in that room.

But why? Why would they have done that? If he is having an affair with her, then he should just leave me. I have been half expecting that anyway, from the moment I realised he had, rightly, stopped loving me.

My ticket to Paris, however I got there, was not paid for from my bank account. That has been a black hole, but Rob explained it away by saying he'd given me the cash.

They would not have taken me by train. They could not have got me on to a plane. That leaves the road. No wonder he was surprised when I said I'd remembered going in a car.

I try to log into his internet banking. He has a separate account from me, and I need to look at it. I have always known his security info, but it doesn't work now. He has, of course, changed it to keep me out. I try to guess things, but they are wrong, and the bank locks me out.

Then I start on his emails. This is easier, as he has left his laptop on. I flick back through the days to last Sunday.

There is nothing remotely suspicious, apart from the fact that none of his few emails mentions that I am not there. If I had taken myself off to Paris for a few days, he should have mentioned it, surely. His internet history is completely clear, which is odd but does not prove anything.

Then I start on the actual paperwork. That is harder, and I know that Rob and Harry will be back soon, but Rob never throws away a piece of paper. If that woman was there to pick up some stuff, he will be coming back to send me away so he can pack it, or whatever needs doing. I race through his files, looking for anything at all that might prove that I am right. That I really did wake up in Paris without any idea of how I got there.

Tucked into the very back of a box file of accounts, folded in half and in half again, I find it. It is a printout of a ferry ticket, booked online.

The date on it is last Monday. During my blackout.

It is a ticket for a minivan to cross from Dover to Calais, with four passengers: three adults and one baby. The names are listed: Robert Hall, Sophie Mayes, Lauren Benjamin and Harry Hall.

I stop, overwhelmed, but knock back the rest of my wine rather than let myself give in now.

That woman is called Lauren Benjamin. She and my partner took my baby to Paris. Harry was part of it. Rob, his girlfriend and Harry drove me to Paris and did whatever they did. And then they came back without me. I check the back of the file: there it is. A return ticket for two adults and an infant. Robert Hall, Lauren

Benjamin and Harry Hall. They sound like a little family. They took me there and came back without me, on Wednesday. On Thursday morning I woke up.

Rob never throws things away. He deletes online, but he hoards paperwork. Thank God.

I hear his key in the door, and fold the two printouts back into quarters and stuff them, for want of a better place, into my bra. As I am putting the file back in its place, they come in.

'Harry!' I say, and I walk towards them, holding my arms out for my baby as he holds his out for me. Rob puts him on the floor, rather than giving him to me, and he crawls straight to me so I pick him up anyway.

'Hey,' says Rob. 'You OK? What are you up to? You look tense.'

'I'm fine.'

I am not going to tell him about the woman. He must know by now. I'll let him worry.

He is looking at my wine glass. 'Drinking? It's only two o'clock.'

I shrug. 'Want a glass?'

He shrugs too. 'OK.'

I pour him a glass of wine and try to work out what on earth I should do next. I go into the bathroom, with Harry, and lock the door. I sit on the floor, which Harry likes, and cuddle him when he flings himself on to my lap, and try to make a plan. I got back from Paris with no money and no ticket. I can get out of this too.

Five minutes later, I know what I have to do, and it is simple. I just have to walk away, with my baby. I stroll into the kitchen and put the dishwasher on, to make it look as if my mind is on the housework.

'I'm just popping out,' I say. Rob will like this, because he must have been going to send me out anyway. Now he will be able to pack his stuff. 'Heading over to Jess's for a little bit.'

He looks up. 'You all right? Are you sure?'

'Of course. Don't worry. I'll get the Tube and I'll only be a couple of hours. Just need a bit of a change of scene, and I want to tell her that stuff I remembered.'

'Course. It's great you remembered. Have fun, then. Get them over for dinner sometime, hey? Arrange a date.'

'Sure.'

I put on my denim jacket, which is darker than Lauren's, and kiss Rob on the mouth, hating it. Then, on my way out of the flat, I pick Harry up from the spot on the sitting-room floor where he is playing with Duplo, and hold him tight.

'Shhh,' I say into his hair. 'Shhh, my darling. Don't make a sound. Mummy's got you.'

Jess is not at home, but Peter is, and he lets us in. I have always liked him.

'Will she be back soon?' I ask. 'I really, really have to see her.'

'I'll call her and find out. She's taking Rose to ballet and Sasha to drama and there are all sorts of tricky things to be done in between times. You know.'

I smile. I don't know. I need my friend. She hasn't always believed in me, but she is the best I have got. Harry is asleep in my arms, and I sit with him heavy on my lap.

'You're a lawyer,' I tell Peter, as he leaves me on the battered sofa and goes to put the kettle on. 'Aren't you?'

'Yes, I am,' he agrees, calling through from the kitchen.

'Don't think I'm mad. All right? But I can't sit here and wait and not say it. Can I tell you something?'

I pull the pieces of paper out of my bra and put them on the table. When he comes back in with two cups of coffee, I start talking.

He listens to my story, and he believes it.

Then he calls Jess and tells her she needs to come home at once.

'Put him upstairs. He can sleep in Rose's bed.' Peter is looking at Harry on my lap. I don't want to let him go, but I know he will be safe there, and I stand up and inhale the smell of his hair. Peter takes the mattress off his four-year-old's bed and puts it on the floor so that Harry will not possibly be able to hurt himself by rolling, and I lower him gently down. He barely stirs. I pull the duvet over him and close the curtains, and we creep out of the room.

When Jess and the girls come rushing back, Peter tells them all to keep quiet, and the girls tiptoe into Rose's room to stare at the sleeping baby.

'You two play in the living room,' Jess tells them firmly, 'and leave him to sleep. The grown-ups need to talk, I think.'

'Very much so,' agrees Peter.

We sit at the table, and the three of us piece it together. Rob turned against me while I was ill, and I barely blame him. He never loved me enough to support me through those kinds of bad times. Since we are not married, he has never made any promises about sticking with me in sickness and in health.

He met Lauren Benjamin somewhere along the line.

When I describe her, with her shiny yellow hair and her double denim, Jess clamps a hand to her mouth.

'Lauren!' she gasps. 'Oh God, no. Lauren! Oh shit.'

'You know her.' I steel myself.

'I introduced them,' she says in a small voice. 'I didn't mean to – I mean, I didn't know. I never thought. Oh God, Sophie. This is terrible.'

'What's terrible? Who is she?'

I watch her and Peter catch each other's eyes. Something passes between them. A door bangs downstairs, but as they live over the top two floors of a big north London house, that happens often. All the same, I am alert.

'I met her at the hospital. In the waiting room,' Jess says slowly. 'You remember, when I had that miscarriage. Not so long ago?'

I nod. I was pregnant with Harry at the time, smug and fertile, and things were difficult for a while between me and Jess. At first it was wonderful that her third child was due at about the same time as my first. Then she lost the baby. She told me not to feel bad about still being pregnant, but I could see it was hard for her.

'The doctors were running very late. I was

there because I'd had problems after losing the baby. I never told you, because you were so busy. Nasty problems, but all sorted now. Lauren was there because she had lost a third pregnancy, and she was being tested for all sorts of dreadful things. We kept in touch, you know, to support each other and all of that.

'It turned out that she had enormous problems and she was never going to carry a baby to term. I think I told you about her once. She and her husband split up.'

I think I am going to be sick. I remember that Jess once mentioned the woman who couldn't carry a baby. She said it to make me feel grateful for Harry.

'She can't have her own child.' I can hardly say this. 'That's why she wants mine.'

The girls are scuffling around, whispering. I hope they are not waking my baby. I want to go and check, but we are all too intent on this conversation. My life is coming apart.

'I introduced her to Rob when you were in hospital. The second time, I mean. After your breakdown. When you were getting better. I told her about you, because of course you were the main thing I was thinking about. We were *so* worried. And she said right away that she wanted to help. So she did. She started helping him out a bit. I thought nothing of it. I thought she was brave, wanting to do that when she was so heartbroken, but I remember saying to Pete that it was probably good for her to have something else to think about. I have no idea how much they saw of each other. Oh God! It never occurred to me for a second. I'm so sorry, Sophie.'

She reaches out and takes my hand. I cannot say anything.

It all makes sense. Rob had fallen utterly out of love with me when I couldn't handle our baby. He had fallen in love, instead, with a woman who had just been told that she would never have a child. He wanted her, not me, and the two of them needed Harry. Rob had always longed to be a father. Lauren could not have a baby. I was a basket case. It must have seemed so simple.

He was giving her my baby. They just needed me out of the way.

'When you got better,' says Peter, working it out as I do, 'it meant you would get custody of him after all. You got better quickly and you were a great mother. Anyone could see that. Suddenly they would have seen that they wouldn't get the baby. Courts prefer the child to be with the mother, and since you were back on your feet and doing so well, they wouldn't have been able to take him from you. They would have wanted you to collapse completely and disown him.'

'They could have had him at weekends and things. The way people do, when they split up.'

Jess sighs. 'I don't think they're that sort of people, are they?'

'But if I look mad and crazy, they'll get to take him for ever.'

'I would imagine so,' says Peter. 'This Paris thing must have been for that. It's an odd plan, but I can see where they were coming from.'

We all look at the pieces of paper, unfolded on the table. The details of it are a blur – they must have drugged me with something strong, got that room from somewhere, and I hate to think of the two of them changing my clothes and just leaving me there – but it is real.

'Sophie,' says Jess. She puts her head in her hands. 'I'm so sorry. I really am. So very, very sorry that I didn't believe you about Paris. You got back here so quickly. That was the most amazing thing to do. And then I accused you of being mad. Because that's what he told me. And that's what I thought. It's such an easy thing to think.'

'Of course it is.'

'Will you forgive me?'

'Of course I will. Don't be silly. I came straight to you, didn't I? The thing is, what do we do now?'

There is something going on outside this kitchen. I stand up to go and see what it is. Something feels wrong.

I open the kitchen door.

Someone runs quickly down the stairs. It is not one of the girls. It is an adult, a woman. It is Lauren Benjamin, and she is holding my baby.

'Harry!' I yell, and he starts to cry, an urgent, high-pitched cry, as if he knows that the wrong thing is happening to him. 'Harry!' I launch myself down the stairs after her. She is faster than me. She is getting away. One of the girls is on the landing, staring, and the other is nowhere to be seen.

'She's got my baby!' I scream, and the woman, Lauren, does not look back, but rushes away, carrying my life in her arms, as fast as she possibly can.

She reaches to open the front door. She pulls it. It rattles, but does not open. She pulls again, harder. Nothing. As I come closer, with Jess and Pete and Rose close behind me, she pulls back the bolts, which have all been shut behind her. The door does not open, and I am there, and Harry is reaching out for me.

Chapter 17

London. Now

It was Rose. Little Rose, aged four, stands in the hallway as we wait for the police, and sucks a strand of her hair.

'I didn't like Lauren any more,' she tells us, as Peter lifts her up and hugs her. 'She wanted to see baby Harry in secret. She said it was a game. I tiptoed down here and did up all the locks.'

I am holding my baby, trying not to think about what would have happened if I'd gone to pick him up and found that he had vanished. I am overcome by the weight of him in my arms, the smell of him, the feeling of his heavy nappy and the warmth of his rosy cheeks. I don't care that Lauren got away after I wrestled Harry from her arms. She finally pulled back the bottom bolt, the one by the floor, and fell down the five steps to the pavement, picked herself up and sprinted across the road.

Our car was parked there, with Rob at the wheel, the engine running. When he saw her coming, Rob started to pull out, pausing just long enough for her to leap in. As they drove off, I saw that she was crying.

'How did she get into the flat, darling?' Jess asked, stroking Rose's hair. 'We didn't hear the buzzer, or we would have gone down.'

'She threw little stones at the window,' says Sasha from behind us. 'We went to look. She was there waving to us, and the top of the window was open so we called down through it. She said to let her in but not to tell any grown-ups because it was a special secret just for us.'

'She threw little stones at the window?' Pete echoes. 'Seriously? How did she know you two would be there, and not us?'

Jess sighs. 'She knew Sophie had come here with Harry. She's been here before. She knows we always sit and talk at the kitchen table. It must have been her only hope. The only thing she could have done. And it nearly worked.'

The front door is still open. As we stand and look out at the sun shining in the wide street, a police car pulls up. I glance at my baby, my little Harry, snug and sleepy in my arms, and I wait to tell my story to people who will, I think, finally believe me.

Books In The Series

Lose yourself
in a good
book with Galaxy®

Curled up on the sofa,
Sunday morning in pyjamas,
just before bed,
in the bath or
on the way to work?

Wherever, whenever,
you can escape
with a good book!

So go on...
indulge yourself with
a good read and the
smooth taste of
Galaxy® chocolate.

Proudly supports

Quick Reads are brilliant short new books written by bestselling writers to help people discover the joys of reading for pleasure.

Find out more at **www.quickreads.org.uk**

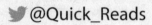 @Quick_Reads  Quick-Reads

We would like to thank all our funders:

LOTTERY FUNDED

We would also like to thank all our partners in the Quick Reads project for their help and support: NIACE, unionlearn, National Book Tokens, The Reading Agency, National Literacy Trust, Welsh Books Council, The Big Plus Scotland, DELNI, NALA

At Quick Reads, World Book Day and World Book Night we want to encourage everyone in the UK and Ireland to read more and discover the joy of books.

World Book Day is on 6 March 2014
Find out more at **www.worldbookday.com**

World Book Night is on 23 April 2014
Find out more at **www.worldbooknight.org**

Why not start a reading group?

If you have enjoyed this book, why not share your next Quick Read with friends, colleagues, or neighbours.

A reading group is a great way to get the most out of a book and is easy to arrange. All you need is a group of people, a place to meet and a date and time that works for everyone.

Use the first meeting to decide which book to read first and how the group will operate. Conversation doesn't have to stick rigidly to the book. Here are some suggested themes for discussions:

- How important was the plot?

- What messages are in the book?

- Discuss the characters – were they believable and could you relate to them?

- How important was the setting to the story?

- Are the themes timeless?

- Personal reactions – what did you like or not like about the book?

There is a free toolkit with lots of ideas to help you run a Quick Reads reading group at **www.quickreads.org.uk**

Share your experiences of your group on Twitter 🐦 @Quick_Reads

For more ideas, offers and groups to join visit Reading Groups for Everyone at **www.readingagency.org.uk/readinggroups**

Other resources

Enjoy this book?

Find out about all the others at **www.quickreads.org.uk**

For Quick Reads audio clips as well as videos
and ideas to help you enjoy reading visit the
BBC's Skillswise website **www.bbc.co.uk/quickreads**

Join the Reading Agency's Six Book Challenge at
www.readingagency.org.uk/sixbookchallenge

Find more books for new readers at
www.newisland.ie
www.barringtonstoke.co.uk

Barrington Stoke

Free courses to develop your skills are available in your
local area. To find out more phone 0800 100 900.

For more information on developing your skills
in Scotland visit **www.thebigplus.com**

Want to read more? Join your local library. You can borrow
books for free and take part in inspiring reading activities.

EMILY BARR

The Sleeper

Lara Finch is living a lie.

Everyone thinks she has a happy life in Cornwall, married to the devoted Sam, but in fact she is desperately bored. When she is offered a new job that involves commuting to London by sleeper train, she meets Guy and starts an illicit affair.

But then Lara vanishes from the night train without a trace. Only her friend Iris disbelieves the official version of events, and sets out to find her.

For Iris, it is the start of a voyage that will take her further than she's ever travelled and on to a trail of old crimes and dark secrets.

For Lara, it is the end of a journey that started a long time ago. A journey she must finish, before it destroys her . . .

Praise for *The Sleeper*:

'Breathless, compulsive reading' Elizabeth Haynes

'Mysterious and intriguing, this thriller is just fabulous' *Closer*

978 0 7553 8800 4

headline
review

Now you can buy any of these other bestselling books by **Emily Barr** from your bookshop or *direct from her publisher*.